מסורה

ArtScroll Youth Series ®

THE DIAMOND BIRD

A Diamond Twins Adventure

THE
DIAMOND

Published by

Mesorah Publications, ltd

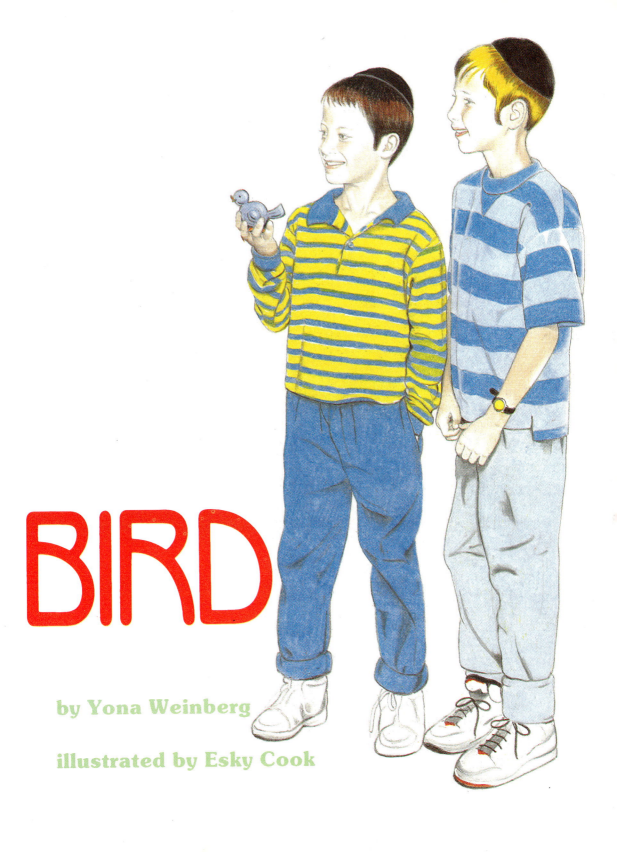

BIRD

by Yona Weinberg

illustrated by Esky Cook

FIRST EDITION
First Impression . . . November, 1991

Published and Distributed by
MESORAH PUBLICATIONS, Ltd.
Brooklyn, New York 11232

Distributed in Israel by
MESORAH MAFITZIM / J. GROSSMAN
Rechov Harav Uziel 117
Jerusalem, Israel

Distributed in Australia & New Zealand by
GOLD'S BOOK & GIFT CO.
36 William Street
Balaclava 3183, Vic., Australia

Distributed in Europe by
J. LEHMANN HEBREW BOOKSELLERS
20 Cambridge Terrace
Gateshead, Tyne and Wear
England NE8 1RP

Distributed in South Africa by
KOLLEL BOOKSHOP
22 Muller Street
Yeoville 2198
Johannesburg, South Africa

ARTSCROLL YOUTH SERIES®
THE DIAMOND BIRD
© Copyright 1991, by YONA WEINBERG and MESORAH PUBLICATIONS, Ltd.
4401 Second Avenue / Brooklyn, N.Y. 11232 / (718) 921-9000

ALL RIGHTS RESERVED.

No part of this book may be reproduced
in any form — *including photocopying and retrieval systems* —
without **written** *permission from the copyright holder,*
except by a reviewer who wishes to quote brief passages in connection with a review
written for inclusion in magazines or newspapers.

THE RIGHTS OF THE COPYRIGHT HOLDER WILL BE STRICTLY ENFORCED.

ISBN:
0-89906-410-8 (hard cover)
0-89906-411-6 (paperback)

Typography by CompuScribe at ArtScroll Studios, Ltd.
4401 Second Avenue / Brooklyn, N.Y. 11232 / (718) 921-9000

Printed in the United States of America by
EDISON LITHOGRAPHING AND PRINTING CORP.
Bound by Sefercraft, Quality Bookbinders, Ltd. Brooklyn, N.Y.

Table of Contents

Chapter 1: Conversations in a Tape 8

Chapter 2: A True Friend 12

Chapter 3: Swords and Dirt 18

Chapter 4: Danger 25

Chapter 5: A Visit to Mr. White 32

Chapter 6: The Play of Life 40

Chapter 7: One of Those Days 45

Chapter 8: Who Stole What from Whom 50

Chapter 9: The Diamond Bird 59

1

Conversations in a Tape

"Cheep! Cheep! Tweet! Tweet! Taka-Taka-Brr..."

The reel turned in the tape recorder, repeating the unusual bird sounds.

"It worked! It worked!" shouted Shaya Diamond, a blond, good-natured eight-year-old, bouncing on his trundel bed.

"Shaya, let's hear more," said Shua, his twin, his dark eyes gleaming with excitement. "I can't believe it. We did it."

An amazing bird had been coming to their tree for the past few weeks. It seemed to be able to mimic the sounds of other birds all night long, becoming more and more persistent and then tapering off just before dawn.

Sometimes the bird sounded like a meadowlark, sometimes a robin or a bluejay, sometimes a skylark or a nightingale. Sometimes it even made the "ribit-ribit" of a frog, or the "rat-tat-tat" of a woodpecker.

The boys tried to get a good look at this bird but whenever they approached the tree, the bird sensed a stranger coming and would stop singing.

"It's the specialest bird I've ever heard," Shua said. He decided to make the bird part of the family. "It's a Diamond bird!"

"And now we've got it on tape," Shaya added proudly. It was his idea to leave a tape recorder outside under the tree all night.

"And now we have a present for Yossi when he comes," Shaya said.

Yossi was their cousin who was coming to spend a few weeks with them while his parents went on a vacation. Yossi was "different" and the boys wanted to give him a special gift, something out of the ordinary.

"Yossi likes birds," said Shaya. "We can't catch this bird, but he can listen to this tape and hear our bird copying the sounds of dozens of other birds."

"Tweet! Tweet! Ka-Loi-Key? Ka-Loi-Key? Yes. . . I think so. . ."

Shaya stared at the tape recorder with his mouth open. "Do you hear what I hear?" he asked.

"I don't know what you hear," said Shua, "but I hear men talking. That bird is amazing. It can even imitate people."

"Wait! Listen!" Shaya yelled. "That's not the bird! Those are real men talking."

". . .can do. . .next week. . ."

"But he might suspect something. . .!"

"Don't worry. That's my job. I've got it all arranged. We'll get in through the basement window. He always leaves it open. . ."

"But that stereo is heavy!"

"The two of us can do it."

"Shaya, those are real men talking and I think they're planning a robbery. But why are they speaking into our tape recorder?" Shua wondered.

"They're not," Shaya figured out. "They didn't see our tape recorder. It was hidden under the pine tree where the bird was. They must've been standing there near the tree and they thought they were alone."

". . .a good time . . . next Tuesday. . . (Tweet! Tweet!) . . . seven o'clock . . ."

"That sounds good. Mr. White will never suspect a thing. (Chirp-Chirp)"

The voices got lower and lower, then faded away, leaving the mockingbird singing its solo.

"Shaya, do you realize what we heard?"

"Yeah!" The recognition slowly dawned on Shaya like a curtain opening up on stage. "There's going to be a robbery next Tuesday at seven o'clock at Mr. White's, of all people."

Mr. White lived down the block from the Diamonds. He had been there for more years than Shua could count.

"Why Mr. White?" wondered Shaya. "He's such a nice man. He gives so much *tzedakah* to our *yeshivah* and he does so much *chesed* and. . ."

"I guess they like his stereo," Shua pointed out.

Shaya swallowed and licked his lips. "We've got to tell somebody about this," he said.

Shua whispered, his quick, impish smile appearing, "You know what I'm thinking, Shaya?" He didn't have to go on. The Diamond twins thought alike. If they could capture those two hoodlums themselves, they'd be heroes.

"Maybe our picture would even be in the paper, and maybe we'd even get a reward!"

Shaya rewound the tape to listen to the voices again. "And Mr. White will be so happy if we saved his stereo."

"Yeah! Especially since he loves music so much."

"But Shaya," Shua remembered, "what are we going to give Yossi now for a present?"

"I don't know. We can't give him this tape. We need it for evidence. Do you think maybe we could capture the bird and give that to him?"

"Nah! We'll never be able to capture our Diamond bird," Shua said. "But we'll think of something. We always do!"

Chapter One: Conversations in a Tape

2

A True Friend

"Mommy! Mommy! They're here!" Aviva called from the front door.

"Hi, Uncle Zevi, Aunt Shani. Hi, Yossi!"

Mrs. Diamond came rushing and hugged her sister. Rabbi Diamond shook hands with Uncle Zevi. "*Shalom Aleichem*, Zev. Good to see you again."

Aviva hung back and stared at Yossi. She was uncomfortable and embarrassed. Although she was a mature ten year old she couldn't speak. She never seemed to know how to act in front of someone like Yossi. She tossed back her caramel colored hair and stared.

Sarale looked at Yossi with her sensitive, kind eyes and smiled. Yossi adjusted his blue cap and returned the smile, his braces gleaming in the sunlight.

Avremele toddled over to Uncle Zevi who scooped him into his arms and lifted him high. "Avremele, you've grown so much since I last saw you!"

"Me big boy!" Avremele reached up and wrapped his arm around Uncle Zevi's neck. He laughed, his dark curls cascading into his face.

"He's two already," Sarale said to Yossi, "and I'm four. How old are you?"

Yossi tilted his head to the side. "I'm ten."

Shua and Shaya came thundering over like like bulldozers, colliding with Uncle Zevi.

"Whoa!" Uncle Zevi put out his hand, as if to stop traffic. "Slow down! My insurance doesn't cover this."

Then the twins offered their hands to Yossi. "*Shalom Aleichem*, Yossi. We're happy that you're going to be staying with us."

Suddenly Shaya said, "C'mon, Yossi, I'll show you my rock collection."

Yossi looked at Shaya shyly. His eyes looked as if his thoughts were far away and he was slowly coming back to the present, as if he were rehearsing in his mind what he was going to say. Then he said, "I collect songs."

"Songs?" both boys shouted.

Yossi did not speak as clearly as the twins and they had to concentrate to understand him. "I like to sing."

"You'll like Mr. White," said Shua. "He collects records. We'll visit him tomorrow if you want."

Yossi nodded. He liked the twins. They didn't treat him differently. He didn't understand why some children didn't want to play with him. Oh, he knew he couldn't do many things as well as other boys. He was slower and it took more effort and patience for him to learn things. But he still had feelings. He felt sad or angry or lonely or happy or excited just like anyone else.

The three boys played in the backyard. "Can you play ball?" Shaya asked.

Yossi tilted his head to the side. "A little," he said. Then he added, "I can't ride a bike, or jump rope, or. . ."

"We'll teach you how to jump rope," Shaya said. "We're the

best jump ropers. . . I mean rope jumpers in our school."

"Yeah," said Shua. "You should see us when we jump rope at *chasunos*. We jump together in front of the *chasan* and everyone claps and cheers and yells."

"I wish I could do that," said Yossi longingly.

"We'll teach you," offered Shaya.

Yossi shook his head from side to side.

"Sure you can do it," Shua said.

"And we'll help you," Shaya added. "With all of us working together, you'll see, I bet you can do it."

That night when the family was sitting around the dining room table eating supper, Yossi announced proudly, "I'm learning how to read from a *Chumash*."

"You are?" said Rabbi Diamond excitedly. He tousled Yossi's hair and winked at the twins. "Maybe Shua and Shaya can take some time out of their busy schedule to help you."

"Oh, Abba," said Shua, "we are going to help Yossi learn lots of important things."

"Oh, really?" Rabbi Diamond looked surprised. "Just make sure it's not something like jumping out of trees."

"Or climbing over fences," added Mrs. Diamond.

"No, we're going to teach Yossi how to jump rope."

"Well, that sounds like fun," said Mrs. Diamond, "and hard work too." She turned to Yossi. "Would you like to learn to jump rope, Yossi?"

Yossi looked at Mrs. Diamond seriously, and said, "I like to jump rope, but I try and can't do it."

"Then I think it's a great idea," said Rabbi Diamond. "What do you think, Aviva?"

Aviva had been sitting quietly. She kept her head down and mumbled, "I guess so."

"Then it's settled," said Mrs. Diamond, "and since rope jumping needs a lot of energy, I make a motion we have extra chocolate pie for dessert."

Rabbi Diamond placed his fist on the table. "I second the motion."

Shua and Shaya jumped up and each shook one of Yossi's hands. "Yippee!"

After supper, Yossi went to his reading lesson. The twins and Aviva were sitting with their parents in the den.

"Abba," Shua began, "why does Yossi look different? Why does he walk like that?"

"And why do his eyes slant upward?" asked Shaya. "And why is he so short? And why. . ."

Rabbi Diamond put his *sefer* down. "You know, boys, that Yossi has Down's syndrome."

"What does that mean?" Shaya asked.

"It means that he was born different from you or me or most people. Something that is easy for you to do, like tying your shoes or buttoning your coat, will always be a major struggle for Yossi."

"Why was he born like that?" Shua asked.

"We don't always know why *Hashem* does certain things," Rabbi Diamond explained. "*Hashem* decided that this child should be born with this specific handicap."

He stopped and stared hard at his boys. "Each person has his own *neshamah* and his own job to accomplish in this world. We can't see the future to know what *Hashem* has in mind for us."

"Can Yossi do *mitzvos* like we do?" Aviva asked.

"Aviva," Rabbi Diamond said, "a person with Down's syndrome

is a complete person. He is just like everyone else and has to serve *Hashem* to his full potential. Having a handicap does not make him less of a person."

Rabbi Diamond stroked his short black beard and continued, "Yossi has the same hopes and joys and disappointments and frustrations as anyone else. Each *neshamah* is placed on earth to perfect itself, and Yossi will learn to serve *Hashem* just like you. But he will do it in his own way, with the abilities *Hashem* gave him."

Shua moved closer to his father. "Maybe, someday, Yossi will wake up and become like everyone else."

"No!" Rabbi Diamond shook his head. "Yossi's problems will never go away. He will never grow out of them like you grow out of a pair of shoes."

"But how come. . ." Shua began.

Mrs. Diamond put her arm around Shua. "The key is not to ask 'how come' or 'why' but 'what can we do to help a child like Yossi to do the best that he can do.' "

"Like teach him to jump rope," said Shua.

"Or ride a bike," said Shaya.

"Or recite *brachos*," said Aviva.

"Or learn to read," suggested Mrs. Diamond.

"Remember," said Rabbi Diamond. "The main thing a boy like Yossi needs is our understanding and sincere caring. Most of all, each one of us needs to learn how to be a true friend to him."

3

Swords and Dirt

Aviva sat up straight, her hands folded neatly on her school desk. She was a sensible girl, orderly and organized. She enjoyed making lists and planning things. Most of all, she enjoyed being at the top of the class.

Now it was time to choose. Every year the fifth grade put on a play. The whole school watched and parents were invited too. Aviva thought happily how she would have the main role. She just knew it. After all, wasn't she the best actress in the class? And Mrs. Miller liked her and she got good grades. Her father was the principal. Mrs. Miller would certainly choose her.

"Okay, class, we'll discuss the play now." Mrs. Miller smiled at twenty eager faces. Aviva looked around. She saw her best friends — Leeba, Rus, and Pesha. They smiled at her. She smiled back. They knew how important it was to her to get the part.

Rus, a very quiet girl, nodded her head and Leeba and Pesha gave their club salute for good luck.

Mrs. Miller continued ...

The play will be about the story of Nachum Ish Gam Zu. He was called by that name because whenever anything happened to him, he always said, *"Gam zu letovah* — this too is for the best."

It happened once that Nachum Ish Gam Zu was sent to Rome to give the king a gift so that he would not make war on the Jewish people. The gift was a chest of precious stones and pearls, and Nachum Ish Gam Zu was chosen because he was a very honest man. On the way, Nachum Ish Gam Zu stopped to rest at an inn.

When the innkeeper saw the strange chest, he became very curious. So after Nachum Ish Gam Zu fell asleep, the innkeeper stole the chest. When he saw what was inside, he removed all the jewels and filled the chest with dirt and pebbles.

The next day, Nachum Ish Gam Zu, unaware of what the inkeeper had done, presented the gift to the king. When the king of Rome opened the box and saw the dirt, he was very angry. He thought the Jews were making fun of him and ordered his soldiers to kill Nachum Ish Gam Zu.

But Nachum Ish Gam Zu was not afraid. He said, *"Gam zu letovah."*

Hashem saw that Nachum Ish Gam Zu had trust in Him, He caused a miracle to happen. When the soldiers threw the dirt into the air, it turned into swords and arrows.

The king was overjoyed with this unique gift. "Now we can conquer our enemies with these weapons," he said, and he rewarded Nachum Ish Gam Zu with a box full of gold and pearls.

Mrs. Miller finished the story and the class waited impatiently for her to give out the parts.

"There are parts for everyone in the class. Rus will be Nachum

20 / The Diamond Bird

Ish Gam Zu; Chavi will be the king; Leah, the innkeeper. . ."

Aviva thought she hadn't heard correctly. "Rus? How could Mrs. Miller choose Rus?" she thought angrily. "Rus is much too quiet and shy. She will never do her part well. Doesn't Mrs. Miller realize that?"

Aviva's anger grew and splintered into sharp fragments. She wanted to speak up in protest, but how could she say anything against her best friend? How could she show her hurt and disappointment? "Surely, Rus herself will turn down the offer," she thought. "She knows how much I want the part, and she would never want to get up on stage to perform."

Aviva glanced at Rus and was surprised by what she saw. Rus' face was red, but she had a small smile on her lips and a glow of pride in her eyes.

Then their eyes met and Rus' smile disappeared. Her face took on a guilty, sad look. She shook her head and whispered loudly enough for Aviva to hear, "I won't take the part if you want it."

Aviva found herself whispering back, "Of course you'll take it. Mrs. Miller chose you. So she must think you'll do a better job than I would."

"Are you sure you really don't mind?" Rus asked.

"Of course, I don't mind. You're my best friend, aren't you? If I can't have the part, then my best friend should."

At recess time, the girls discussed the play. "That's so nice of you, Aviva," Leeba said.

"You really don't mind Rus' having the main part?" Pesha asked.

"No," Aviva said quietly, "but I wish Mrs. Miller didn't make me the announcer."

Leeba agreed. "Mrs. Miller said she wanted someone who

speaks clearly and with expression to be the announcer. But it does seem a dull part for you, Aviva."

"I wouldn't do my part if you minded," Rus spoke softly, "but I'm glad you don't. I've never had a main part in a play before. My parents will be so proud. I'm so happy and scared at the same time."

"Maybe you'll be too scared to act," Aviva wanted to say. But she reproached herself for her unkind thoughts.

Would Nachum Ish Gam Zu have felt this way? Aviva thought. He believed that everything that happened to him was for the best. Would he have been miserable like she was because something didn't work out the way he wanted it to?

"I have to go now. I'm baby-sitting," Aviva said.

"We can come to your house later, Aviva," suggested Leeba, "and discuss the play."

Aviva didn't want her friends coming to her house. It wasn't the play she was worrying about now. It was Yossi. She didn't want her friends to meet him. What if he embarrassed her walking and talking in his awkward way?

"Okay," she said, not knowing else what to do. "Let's meet in an hour."

The four girls walked home together, one of them with a very heavy heart.

"Whatsamatter?" asked Sarale, when she saw her sister looking upset.

"I didn't get the part I wanted in the play." Aviva said.

"Are you angry?" asked Yossi.

Aviva turned and looked at her cousin. He understood. "Yes, I'm angry," she confessed. "But I'm angry that I'm angry."

Yossi nodded. "Sometimes I get sad," he said slowly. "Then I get sad because I'm sad."

"Do you want a cookie?" Sarale asked.

"No, thank you," Aviva said kindly. "You kids go find Avremele and play. The girls are coming over soon and we have things to discuss."

"Okay," Sarale answered cheerfully. Yossi and she left the kitchen, leaving Aviva sitting by the table with her head in her hands.

4

Danger

Sarale put her beloved, tattered, stuffed animal into Avremele's hands. "Her name is Vivi," she said loudly.

Avremele laughed and hugged the bear tightly. "Vivi," he repeated. Sarale nodded.

Yossi lined his pennies in a straight row on the floor and watched Sarale and Avremele playing.

"And this is Min-min," Sarale announced. She placed the stuffed monkey next to Avremele. "Min-min is a monkey."

"Mon-kee."

"Right! You hold Min-min and I'll go get something for us to eat." Avremele laughed and clapped his hands.

Sarale went to the kitchen to prepare some snacks.

"Sarale," Aviva said, appearing in the kitchen doorway. "I'm going to walk my friends to the corner. We want to discuss our play. You watch Avremele, okay? I'll be right back."

"Okay," Sarale understood. Aviva was baby-sitting for them and now she, Sarale, was in charge for a few minutes.

Sarale poured some milk from the heavy container into the plastic cups. She spilled some milk on the table which dribbled onto the floor.

"Oh, no!" she cried. She quickly took a towel and wiped up the mess. Then she pushed a chair next to the counter, climbed on it, and took down a box of crackers and a bag of popcorn. She had been preparing snacks for about ten minutes when Yossi came walking into the kitchen in his awkward way. His face was twisted into a frown.

"Sarale, Sarale," he stammered.

"I'm coming soon," Sarale said and continued with her preparations.

"No! No!" Yossi pulled Sarale's arm.

"Let me go, Yossi. I said I'm coming soon." Sarale was getting

upset. Yossi persisted. He was upset too. He pulled and pulled until Sarale finally followed him. "Okay, I'm coming."

Yossi pulled her quickly. He seemed agitated and distressed about something.

"Avremele," he said, breathing quickly. "Avremele did something bad."

Sarale stared at Yossi's face. She understood that something was wrong.

"Where's Avremele?" she asked. Yossi took her hand and walked as quickly as he could to her parents' bedroom.

Sarale saw Avremele standing by the dresser, a big smile on his face. Nothing was wrong. What was Yossi trying to tell her? Then Yossi pointed to Avremele's hand. Sarale didn't understand, but she knew the meaning of an empty medicine bottle. It meant danger.

"Avremele, did you eat the medicine in the bottle?"

"Me eat good me-cine," Avremele answered truthfully.

"Yossi," Sarale said. "You watch Avremele. I'll go get Aviva."

She didn't know what needed to be done, but she knew she had to place the responsibility on someone older and wiser than she was.

She ran to the door and called, "Aviva! Aviva!" There was no answer. "Aviva! Aviva!" But Aviva was nowhere to be seen.

Sarale rushed back to the house. What should she do?

"Telephone," Yossi stammered. But whom could she call? She went to the telephone and dialed zero. She had once seen her mother do that.

"Operator. May I help you?" the voice on the other end of the phone spoke.

28 / *The Diamond Bird*

"Avremele ate the whole bottle of medicine. I don't know what to do."

"Wait, I'll give you Poison Control."

"Poison Control speaking."

Sarale repeated her story.

"How old is he?"

"He's two."

"How much does he weigh?"

"I don't know, but he's heavy when I pick him up."

"Little girl, what is your name?"

"Sarale."

"Sarale, how old are you?"

"I'm four. I'll be five on *Sa-vuos*."

"Sarale, is there any grown-up at home with you? Your mother? Your father? An older sister or brother?"

"No, Aviva went out and I can't find her."

"Sarale, do you know your address?"

"Sure, I have two Shabbos dresses, a pink one and a red one."

"Do you have any neighbors near you?"

"Yes, my friend Shoshy lives next door to me."

"Sarale, listen carefully. You go next door to Shoshy's house and speak to her mother. Tell her to come quickly to the phone. I'll wait here. But you have to hurry. It's very important. Do you understand?"

"Yes." Sarale didn't understand exactly what the lady said. She just knew it was important and she had to hurry.

Shoshy's mother was at home. She rushed next door to the phone and Sarale watched as the older woman took over.

Aviva returned a few minutes later to find an ambulance ready to take Avremele to the hospital. A cold shiver shook her. She felt a rising sense of panic. She clapped her hand over her mouth.

Later that evening, with Avremele sleeping safely in his crib and the danger past, Aviva burst out crying.

"It was all my fault, Mommy," she sobbed. "I was talking to the girls about the play and I forgot the time."

Mrs. Diamond had her arms around Aviva and her face was pale and exhausted.

"*Baruch Hashem*, everything turned out all right. Thank goodness, Yossi understood the danger and Sarale had the good sense to do what she did quickly."

"But, Mommy, if anything would have happened, I would have been the one to blame."

"It's over now, *Mamale*, and I see that you understand. I'm sure in the future you will never let something like this happen again. This was a lesson with *rachamim* because of the way it turned out. All we can do now is try to learn from our mistakes."

Later, before Aviva went to sleep, she sat on Sarale's bed, watching her sleeping sister. She looked like a sleeping doll with her blond, unruly curls falling on her small face.

"I'm sorry, Princess," Aviva whispered. "And thank you. I love you."

She kissed Sarale's soft cheek and the four-year-old smiled in her sleep.

5

A Visit to Mr. White

"C'mon, Yossi, jump!" the twins yelled. Each boy stood at one end turning the rope as Yossi tried to jump.

They had been practicing for a long time and it was becoming a tedious job. Yossi's low muscle tone and poor sense of balance were making it almost impossible.

"I can't!" Yossi thought. He breathed hard, and sweat poured down his forehead. He turned the cap around on his head with the brim facing the back.

He tried again. This time he took the rope, held it tightly in his hands and swung it over his head. By the time the rope reached the ground Yossi's legs were tangled in it like a fish in a net.

He tried again and again. His right foot stomped on the rope. Then his left. Then he tripped and fell.

Shua approached Yossi, helped him up and put his arm around his shoulders. "You can do it, Yossi!"

Yossi shrugged off Shua's arm and threw the rope down in disgust.

His mouth turned down in a frown and a few tears of frustration formed in his eyes.

Shua felt puzzled and hurt. Why was Yossi angry at him? He was only trying to help.

Shaya understood. "Shua," he said, "Remember that time you were learning to play basketball?"

Shua remembered. He had been in day camp and all the boys were throwing the ball into the basket as easy as rolling dice.

As hard as he had tried he just couldn't do it. Yudie, his counselor, had kept on shouting, "C'mon, Shua, don't give up! You can do it!" But, when he still couldn't throw the ball, Shua had been so frustrated and angry he had quit the game.

"Wanna take a break?" asked Shua. "Let's visit Mr. White and practice later again."

Yossi agreed. Anything was better than this exhausting struggle.

"C'mon, let's go," said Shaya. "We'd better change into clean clothes first."

Mr. White opened his door with a big smile. He was a tall man with a pleasant face and slightly stooped shoulders.

"*Kumt arain! Kumt arain!* How nice to see my best friends. You're just in time to share my snack of...uh...cookies and milk."

The boys sat around the kitchen table and Mr. White brought fruit and store-bought cookies to the table. Then he poured milk for all of them.

"So, what new mischief have you boys been up to?"

"Well, you should hear our tape..." Shaya began. Shua kicked him. "Ow! What did you do that for? Oh, yeah! No! No! There's nothing new, Mr. White. How's your stereo doing?"

"My stereo?" Mr. White lifted his eyebrows in surprise. "Well, now that you mention it, it hasn't been working well lately. You know how much I love music, especially *chasunah* records and boys' choirs, like *Yaldei Chain*. Maybe I'll buy a new stereo someday."

Yossi leaned his chin on his upturned palm. "I like to sing," he announced.

"You do? What do you sing?" asked Mr. White.

Yossi responded by singing a few songs he had learned. He sang loudly, with gusto.

When he finished, all three clapped loudly.

"*Zeese yingele!*" Mr. White beamed.

Yossi smiled with pleasure and pride. He fixed his cap and pushed the brim to the back again. It felt so good to be praised and admired.

"I know what *brachah* to make on a peach," Yossi added as he picked up the fuzzy fruit. He made the *brachah,* pronouncing each word carefully and slowly.

"That was a beautiful *brachah,*" said Mr. White.

After their nosh, they all went into the living room.

"Yossi," Shua pointed out. "Your shoelace is undone. Shall I tie it for you?"

Yossi looked down at his feet. He bent forward slowly. "I can do it," he said proudly.

With much effort, Yossi pulled the strings together and carefully and slowly tied them in a bow. It had taken him a long time to learn this skill.

"Hey! That's great, Yossi!" Shua shouted. "You're okay, pal." He slapped Yossi on the back affectionately.

"What's that?" Yossi pointed to a smooth, polished object on the mantelpiece.

Mr. White took down a small, carved, wooden *Sefer Torah.*

"Please tell Yossi the story of the little Torah," Shaya began. The twins had heard the story many times but enjoyed hearing it again. Their eyes shone whenever they touched the old, wooden carving. "I wish we had something like this," Shua once said. Of all the toys they had, none was as beautiful and meaningful as the little, golden-brown Torah, worn with age.

Mr. White settled back on his couch:

When I was a little boy. . .oh. . .about your age. . .I lived in a little *shtetl* in Poland. My father was a *talmid chacham* who studied Torah all day, and my mother was a great *tzadaikes*. We were a very poor but very warm, happy family.

In our *shul,* there lived a *shamas* who was very old and

couldn't see well. He had a funny way of walking, but he could carve the most beautiful objects with his small knife and a piece of wood.

I often watched him sitting outside the *shul* whittling away at a piece of wood till it took on a life of its own. One time, I watched with amazement as the wood in his hands took on the shape of a small, open *Sefer Torah*. Ah. . .how I wished I could own such a work of art, carved with such care and love.

The *shamas* was a quiet man and hardly spoke to anyone. Some boys in our *shtetl*, I'm sorry to say, were not kind. They made fun of our old *shamas* and often played tricks on him. I always greeted him with a friendly "good-morning" and a cheery smile.

One summer day, the boys were looking for mischief. They decided to play a trick on our innocent *shamas*.

Four strong boys pulled and rolled a huge rock right in front of the entrance to the *shul*. They knew the *shamas* would try to move it away and not succeed.

I watched them do it but I was too scared to stop them. They were older and stronger than I.

That night, I quickly ran to the *shul*. I was small for my age, but with all my strength, I heaved and pushed and pulled that rock till I was covered with black-and-blue bruises on my legs and bleeding scrapes on my arms. But I managed to remove the rock from the doorway.

Chapter Five: A Visit to Mr. White / 37

I ran back home feeling good.

The next morning, on my way out to *shul*, I found this on my doorstep.

[Mr. White then lifted the wooden *Sefer Torah*]. It was newer and cleaner then, but otherwise, it's still the same.

Inside, were printed the words. *"Tzu der yingel vass farshtait vee tzu tun kavod habrios"* — To the young boy who knows how to give respect to other people.

There was no signature. But there was only one man in our town who could produce a work of art of this kind.

I ran to the *shul* to thank the *shamas* for his gift but he pretended he didn't know what I was talking about.

"He wanted to keep his *mitzvah* a secret," Shaya said.

"Yes, I believe you're right. He was a quiet man and kept his deeds quiet. I believe he was a *tzaddik* who did a lot of *mitzvos* secretly."

"He didn't want to brag about what he did," Shua added.

Mr. White sat forward, the little wooden Torah in his lap. "This little Torah taught me a valuable lesson for all my life. It taught me to understand the meaning of *kavod habrios*.

"We're all *Hashem's* children, each and every one of us, and *Hashem* wants us to respect and love one another. Each person has his own special goodness in him and we need to search and find that good in each person. There is no one without some value, some unique quality that makes him special.

"To respect and love *Hashem's* creatures . . . that is what this little Torah has taught me."

"You know what it taught me?" asked Shua.

"What, *Yingele?*"

Shua smiled brightly. "That when I grow up I'm going to be such a big *tzaddik* and do so much *chesed* and *mitzvos* and I'm not going to tell anybody about it. I'm going to do it quietly, and nobody — and I mean NOBODY — is going to know about it."

"But you just told us," Shaya said, "so we know!"

"Oh . . .uh . . . okay! But you don't tell anybody about it, okay?"

"Okay!"

Shua looked longingly at the wooden *Sefer Torah*. "I wish I could carve like that," he said.

"I wish I could fly," said Shaya.

"I wish I could jump rope," said Yossi.

Mr. White looked amused. "What do you wish, Mr. White?" Shaya asked.

"Me?" Mr White winked. "I wish all little *Yiddishe kinderlach* would be as *zeese* and kind and caring and considerate as you *boychiks*."

6

The Play of Life

The auditorium was crowded. Aviva watched from behind the curtain. She could see her mother and her friends in the back.

"Wow! Look how many people came to see our play!" she exclaimed.

"I am so nervous," said Leeba.

"Me, too," said Rus with a tremor in her voice. She twirled a brown curl around and around her finger. "I don't feel so good."

Aviva looked at her. Yes, Rus didn't look too well. Her face had a greenish tinge to it and she looked like Aviva did when she was sick with a virus.

"Are you scared?" Aviva asked.

Rus nodded and laughed a high squeaky laugh which revealed her tension.

"Well, no wonder!" Aviva said. "There must be a thousand people out there!"

Rus' eyes opened wide in horror. Suddenly, Aviva had a plan. If Rus became too scared to act, who would take her place? Why, she, Aviva, who knew Rus' part better than anyone else in the class.

Why, she...no, that wasn't right. The play meant too much to Rus.

She opened her mouth to comfort Rus, but surprised herself by saying, "I know someone who was so scared, she fainted right on stage, in front of everyone! They had to pull her off stage like a sack of potatoes. They..."

She didn't finish. Suddenly, Rus put her hand to her mouth and ran away.

Aviva stared. Well, if Rus was so terrified, she couldn't do anything about it. Some people were just not made for this sort of thing.

It was a good thing acting in front of an audience didn't scare her. She was brave and confident. She always had been. She knew she wouldn't make any mistakes, and could speak loudly and clearly with plenty of expression.

"Aviva," a voice behind her interrupted her thoughts. Aviva turned around to see her teacher, Mrs. Miller.

"I'm afraid we have a problem." Aviva looked at her with hopeful eyes. "Rus is not feeling well. She seems to have a very bad case of stage fright. Do you think you could take over?"

Aviva couldn't believe her good luck. Did she think she could take over?

"Yes, Mrs. Miller," she said politely, keeping her bubbly excitement hidden.

"Good! I was sure I could count on you. I know you know her part very well. You've been at all the rehearsals and I've heard you coach all the other girls. Go to the dressing room and change costumes with Rus. But hurry! We're due to start soon."

Aviva was ecstatic. She knew it! Finally, she would have a chance to prove what a fabulous actress she was. Her mother would be so proud of her! Wasn't she the star pupil of the class? Now she would be a real star on stage.

Aviva found Rus in the dressing room sobbing and hiccuping in the corner. She looked up at Aviva with a tear-stained face.

"I'm sorry, Aviva," she cried. "I just can't do it. I'm too (hic) scared."

Aviva looked at Rus with compassion. Rus had wanted to be in the play so badly. It was the first time she had *ever* been chosen for the leading role. Her mother and father were out there, too. What would they think?

All of life is like a play, Aviva thought, and all the people in it are the actors. Each generation has its own settings, its own scenes, its own actors, and *Hashem* is the Producer and the Director.

Aviva sighed.

But. . .

Each person is given the choice how to act in "the play."

Hashem is the final judge of how well each person performs.

Aviva chewed on her lower lip. "Rus, it's really not as bad as you think."

"Oh, sure!" Rus retorted. "You, yourself, told me you knew someone who fainted on stage."

"Yes," said Aviva. "But you know what? After they gave her some water, she returned to the stage and did a great job!"

"Really?"

"Yes."

"But I just can't, Aviva. I . . ."

"Sure you can," Aviva coaxed her. "I've seen you act, Rus. You're good. You'll see. You get out there and forget about the audience. Just remember that you're Nachum Ish Gam Zu and do your part."

Chapter Six: The Play of Life / 43

"Do you really think so, Aviva?"

"I know so, Rus. I wouldn't say it if I didn't mean it."

Rus smiled. "Aviva, if you feel I can do it, maybe I can."

"Go ahead, Rus. You're the star."

The two girls looked at each other intently. Aviva couldn't speak. She felt like something was stuck in her throat.

The play was a hit. Aviva heard the applause Rus received as she came to take her bow.

"That could have been for me." She brushed away a tear. No, that applause was *not* meant for her. It was meant for Rus, and no one was going to see her cry like a baby. This was her secret. She would tell no one about it. It was just between her and *Hashem*.

If Nachum Ish Gam Zu were here, Aviva thought, he'd probably be proud of me. He'd probably say, "Aviva, you're a great kid. And you know what?... *Gam zu letovah!*"

7
One of Those Days

Officer Thomas knew it was going to be a bad day. As soon as he woke up and stubbed his toe walking to the kitchen, he knew. Then he scalded himself while pouring a cup of coffee, burned his toast, and couldn't find his car keys.

He called the police captain at the station. "I'm going to be a little late," he said.

"Anything wrong?" the captain asked.

"No, no," said Officer Thomas, rummaging through his drawers for his keys. "Just one of those mornings. That's all!"

"Well, don't worry," said the captain. "Things are pretty quiet here today. Nothing much happening."

"That's good! I can use a normal day for a change," said Officer Thomas as he hung up.

After finally finding his keys, Officer Thomas got into his car and drove to the station.

The car radio buzzed: *"Six-Charlie-32 Respond."*

Officer Thomas pushed a button and answered, "Six-Charlie-32-here go ahead!"

"There's a '61 Plymouth brown vehicle stalled on route 16. One mile east of Exit 7. Vehicle number 2341. Elderly couple. Need help. Stalling traffic."

Officer Thomas answered, "I'm on my way. 10-4." He pressed

his foot down on the gas pedal and zoomed ahead. Things were beginning to pick up.

Braang! Phttt! Zang!

"Oh no! What was that?" His car was slowing down . . . slower . . . slower . . . Officer Thomas pushed his foot hard on the gas pedal till his veins showed purple in his neck.

ZZTT! Chug . . . Chug . . . His car stopped!

"Now, what?" He spoke aloud through gritted teeth.

He got out of the car, walked to the front, lifted the hood, and peered in.

"Hmmm . . . Hmm . . . " He rubbed his nose and stared. He stared . . . and stared . . . and stared. Repairing cars was one thing Officer Thomas knew very little about. Oh, he knew how to drive a car well, and even to change a tire occasionally. But when it came to knowing how the engine worked, he was at a loss.

"Well, there's only one thing left to do," he thought. "I'd better call for help."

He went back into his car and turned on the two-way radio.

"Six-Charlie-32 calling base. Six-Charlie-32 calling base."

"Go ahead 32!"

"I need your help. You see the car stopped and . . ."

"I know! The car is still waiting for you. Why aren't you there already? I told you, they're an elderly couple and they need help. What's taking you so long?" The dispatcher sounded angry.

Officer Thomas answered, "I'm trying to tell you. The car is stuck!"

"I know that the car is stuck! That's why we asked you to get over there."

"No! No!"

"Yes! Yes!"

"No, I mean *my* car is stuck! My car stopped working. I don't know what's wrong with it. I need help."

There was a long pause on the other end. Finally, *"I don't believe this. I'll send you someone."* Click!

Officer Thomas leaned against his car and watched the passing traffic. He was causing a jam on the highway. People were slowing down in their cars to stare at him.

After a few moments another police car stopped. Then another. And another. With their red lights flashing and turning it looked like a police car parade.

"Officer Thomas, what's wrong with your car?" asked one of the policemen.

"I don't know, but look at this bottleneck we're causing. Let's get the car to the shoulder."

All the policemen went to the back of the car and together they heaved and pushed.

Slowly . . . slowly . . . slowly . . . like ants moving a beetle, they rolled the car to the side.

Car after car slowed down to watch this unusual spectacle of eight burly, strong policemen rolling a police car down the road.

When the police car was safely parked on the shoulder, the other policemen drove away.

"We'll send you a tow truck right away!"

"Thanks!"

Officer Thomas sat in his hot, stuffy car and waited . . . and waited . . . and waited.

"Why doesn't a tow truck ever come when you need it?" he fumed. He took out his handkerchief and wiped his wet face.

"Whew! What a day! What a day! I wonder what else is in store for me today?"

Chapter Seven: One of Those Days / 47

He looked up at the hot sun. It was high in the middle of the cloudless sky.

"It's only noon and I've just about had it for today. I hope the captain won't be too angry with me."

It was an hour later when a tow truck finally came to assist him.

Officer Thomas drove down to the station hoping there would be no more surprises in store for him.

"Officer Thomas reporting, Sir!"

The captain looked up from his papers on his desk. "Well, it's about time. What happened to you?"

As Officer Thomas approached the desk he stubbed his big toe on a bench.

"Ow!" he yelled, hopping on one foot.

It was the same toe he had hurt that morning.

"The tow truck . . . the tow truck came . . ." he began. He looked up. The captain was laughing.

"Toe truck? Did you say toe truck?"

Oh, no! Officer Thomas was in no mood for the captain's kind of humor now.

"Ahem!" The captain was in control again. "Okay! Let's just forget about it. By the way, your elderly couple is fine. A passing gray Oldsmobile stopped and two young men with black hats got out and helped them."

"Great!" thought Officer Thomas. Why didn't they stop and help him too?

"All right!" The captain's voice was all business.

"Now, for your next assignment. Do you think you're quite ready for it?"

Officer Thomas straightened up to his full five feet ten inches and said confidently, "YES, SIR!"

"All right! We received a report of a robbery."

"Where?"

"Well . . . " the captain hesitated. "You see . . . it . . . uh . . . hasn't happened yet."

Officer Thomas removed his cap and scratched his head. "Oh, Brother," he muttered. "I knew I should have stayed in bed this morning." Then he added, "Tell me, Captain how'd you discover this unhappened robbery?"

"Well," said the captain, "a few minutes ago I got this call . . . but . . . you'll never believe this."

Officer Thomas rolled his eyes. "Captain, with the kind of day I'm having, I'm just about ready to believe anything!"

8

Who Stole What from Whom

"Hello! Hello! I'd like to report a robbery," Shaya yelled into the phone.

"No! I can't tell you my name but I just want to warn you to keep your men handy tonight at seven o'clock at 614 Smoketree Road. Yes, that's right. A robbery. Somebody's going to steal a stereo. I'm giving you a warning. That's all. Good-bye and good luck." Click!

"Well, we did it!" Shaya said. "Now we've got to make our plans to be there when those thieves get caught."

Shua and Shaya walked along the sidewalk in the warm afternoon sun and tried not to step on any cracks. The day seemed to drag by.

The twins decided to spend the afternoon practicing rope jumping with Yossi again. They had been doing it every day since Yossi had come for his visit.

"One. . .two. . .hmph. . ."

"Yossi, you're getting better, you know!" said Shua.

"Too hard!" Yossi complained.

"But you can do it," the twins persisted. "C'mon, Yossi, try it again."

"Can't."

"Yossi!" Shaya opened his blue eyes wide. "Think of all the

people at *chasunos* who will clap for you when you jump in front of the *chasan*."

Yossi smiled and jumped.

"One...two...hmph...no more!"

"C'mon, Yossi, c'mon!" Both twins jumped excitedly, encouraging their cousin.

Yossi huffed and jumped for well over an hour till the twins decided to quit for the day.

Seven o'clock finally came and the boys ran to Mr. White's house. They hid behind the clump of bushes that stretched out in front of Mr. White's house. They kept themselves down low and peered through the bushes.

Crickets, frogs and locusts hummed and buzzed in the woods behind the yard. The garden was alive with rich colors.

SCRATCH! SCRATCH!

"What was that noise?" Shaya opened his eyes wide.

"Are you scared?" Shua asked nervously.

"I. . .don't know. But maybe this wasn't such a good idea after all."

SCRATCH! SCRATCH! Brr. . .Br. . .ow! Something soft and furry flashed by, brushing Shaya's leg. "YIKES! A tiger! Let's get outta here!"

"It's only a cat!" Shua laughed. Shaya laughed, too. "A cat? I really knew that. I was just kidding."

Soon the boys noticed a gray Oldsmobile parked in front of the house. At first, there didn't seem to be anything unusual about it, but after ten minutes, when the passengers made no move to get out, the twins became suspicious.

"Whose car is that?" Shaya wondered. "It looks familiar," said Shua.

Two young men eventually emerged. They walked to the back of the car and opened the door.

"Look!" Shaya forgot to whisper. "It looks like Mr. White's stereo is in there."

"They stole it already?" Shaya whined. "We missed all the action. Now what are we going to do?"

"Sh . . . listen!" Shua pulled Shaya farther back.

"I've never done anything like this before, you know!" said one of the men.

"Me, neither," said the other, "but we've got a job to do, so let's do it."

"Uh. . .oh!" Shaya squinched up his nose. "Not now, nose. Be good. Not now. If I squeeze my nose real tight then I won't. . .I won't. . .AH-CHOO!"

"What was that?" asked one of the men.

"It's just a cat," Shaya whispered back. "Meeow. . .Meeow," he began.

"Strange-sounding creature. Let's go before I get cold feet!"

The men walked to the side of Mr. White's house, leaving the car's back door open.

"C'mon, Shua," Shaya hissed frantically. "Now's our chance. We'll take the stereo and return it to Mr. White."

Shua followed, his heart pounding. The boys dashed to the car and tried to lift the heavy stereo. Shua gasped. They finally managed to lift the stereo and huffing and puffing and grunting managed to carry it to their hiding place behind the bushes.

No sooner were they hidden than the two men returned just as a police car came zooming by.

"It's gone!" shouted the men. "Someone took our stereo. We've been robbed."

The policeman was getting out of his car. "Where's the robbery?" he asked.

Shua and Shaya jumped out of the bushes. "Here's the robbery!" they shouted, pushing the stereo out.

The two men stared at the twins, who seemed to have come out of nowhere, and saw the stereo.

"You stole our stereo!" they shouted.

"They stole this stereo!" the twins shouted.

"Who stole what stereo?" the policeman shouted.

In the meantime, several cars were parking and people were approaching the scene.

Chapter Eight: Who Stole What from Whom / 53

"What's going on here?" asked an older man.

"There's been a robbery," explained the policeman. "But I still haven't figured out who did what to whom."

"They're the robbers," shouted the two men, together with the twins, pointing at each other.

Some of the bystanders started muttering among themselves.

"A robbery! There's been a robbery!"

"A what?"

"A robbery!"

"Where? What? When? Who?"

"He did it!"

"They did it!"

"You did it!"

"HOLD IT!" yelled the policeman. "Now, one at a time. You! What's your name?"

"Shaya."

"What's your name?"

"Shua."

"What's your name?"

"Chaim Willner."

"What's your name?"

"Moish Itzkowitz."

"What's your name?" asked Shaya.

"Officer Thomas. But my friends call me Tom . . . WAIT A MINUTE! I'll ask the questions. Now! Can one of you please tell me who this stereo belongs to."

Mr. White, who had heard all the racket, was coming out of his house. He stopped and stared at all the people. "What's going on here?"

Suddenly, it was very quiet. Everyone looked at Mr. White.

For a few seconds no one moved. Then one person shouted, "Surprise!" and everyone joined in. People rushed over to Mr. White and shook his hands. *"Mazel Tov! Mazel Tov!"*

The two young men shouted too, *"Mazel Tov!"* Officer Thomas turned from one face to another. He shook his head and looked perplexed. "I knew I should have stayed in bed this morning."

Shua and Shaya swung their heads back and forth. People were smiling and laughing and shaking hands. What was going on here? What kind of a robbery was this, anyway?

"Mr. White, isn't this your stereo?" Shaya asked.

"My stereo? What's going on here?"

"That's what I've been trying to figure out," said Officer Thomas as he drummed his fingers on his belt.

"It's yours, Mr. White," Chaim and Moish smiled.

"You see," Shaya shouted, "they did steal it."

"Of course, we didn't steal it," said Moish Itzkowitz. "We bought it and we were going to sneak it into Mr. White's house through the basement window before you kids took it. It's a present for his anniversary."

Anniversary? Everyone started shouting again. *"Mazel tov! Mazel tov!"*

"Anniversary?" Shaya and Shua stared at each other.

"Whose anniversary is it?" asked Officer Thomas. He felt as if he were participating in a very mixed-up dream.

"Mr. White's," explained Chaim. "He's been living in our town for fifty years, and has done so much good for so many of us that the people in our community wanted to do something special for him to show our appreciation. So we were planning to make him a surprise party tonight."

"Oh, my!" said Mr. White.
"Oh, no!" said the twins.
"Oh, Brother!" said Officer Thomas.

9

The Diamond Bird

The next day, Mr. White couldn't stop laughing. He was sitting in his kitchen with Rabbi and Mrs. Diamond and their family and Yossi. The twins had just finished explaining about the tape and their bird and the so-called robbery.

"This is too much...too much...," said Mr. White as he held his stomach and tried to stop laughing. "I haven't had so much fun since...since..."

"Since the twins gave you a mouse for a pet?" suggested Rabbi Diamond. That set Mr. White off on another laughing fit.

Avremele and Sarale sat quietly eating ice cream and cake. They enjoyed being with the grown-ups where they felt loved and safe and happy.

Aviva and Mrs. Diamond were cleaning in the kitchen, while the twins were sweeping the floors in the dining room.

"It was a great party last night," said Aviva.

"Yes," said Mrs. Diamond. "I'm glad it turned out well, considering the excitement it started off with."

She shook her head and chuckled. "Those boys really know how to turn a trickle into a river."

Aviva laughed. "Or a party into a robbery."

Yossi had wandered off into the utility room. There were so many interesting things here for a boy to explore. Boxes and tools, a flashlight, a tape measure, and...a rope!

Yossi's eyes rested on the rope for a few seconds, and then he picked it up.

"Look, Mommy!" Aviva called. "Look what Yossi's doing!"

Her shout brought the others from the kitchen. Mr. White, Rabbi Diamond, Mrs. Diamond, Aviva, Shua and Shaya, Sarale and Avremele all stood at the doorway staring at the boy with Down's syndrome who was jumping rope.

"ONE...TWO...THREE...FOUR..." Yossi huffed as he swung the rope around and around.

"I can't believe it." Mrs. Diamond had tears in her eyes.

Rabbi Diamond shook his head in wonderment. "You see what a little hard work and perseverance can do."

Mr. White smiled warmly. *"Zeese yingele! Zeese yingele!"* he said.

Yossi stopped jumping and smiled at his audience.

Mrs. Diamond rushed over to him and hugged him tightly. "Oh, Yossi, Yossi," she whispered.

"Shua and Shaya helped me," Yossi said. "We practiced every day. It was hard work. Now I can jump rope at *chasunos* just like Shua and Shaya, and everybody will clap for me." It was the longest speech Yossi had made since he had come to the Diamonds.

Rabbi Diamond came over and shook Yossi's hand firmly. "Yossi, we're very proud of you."

"I think we need some music," said Mr. White, as he went to play one of his favorite records on his new stereo. He returned with a small object in his hands. "Shua and Shaya," he said proudly, "Someone once gave me this because he felt I deserved it. I now give it to you because I *know* you earned it."

It was the little wooden *Sefer Torah*. For once, the twins were speechless. Then Shaya recovered. "Boy! Thanks, Mr. White. This is the specialest present we've ever had."

Shua fumbled for something in his pocket. "We have a present for you, Yossi. I almost forgot about it. We wanted to give you one when you came, but it took us a while to figure out what you'd appreciate."

The twins approached Yossi. "We hope you like it," said Shaya. They handed him a little glass figure in the shape of a bird.

"We know you like birds," said Shua.

"We wanted to buy you a Diamond bird," said Shaya, "like the one that sang in our tree."

"But we didn't have enough money," said Shua.

"Then we wanted to buy you a *real* diamond bird," said Shaya.

"But we didn't have enough money," said Shua.

"My bird!" Yossi said. To him the bird was no less precious than a real diamond one, and he knew he would always treasure it.

The twins could see the love that glowed in Yossi's eyes. It was as if he had a lighted candle somewhere inside him.

Yossi looked at the twins, a giant smile on his face. "You're nice!"

Aviva looked at Yossi and thought about how much things had changed since he first came. She liked Yossi now and was not embarrassed by him anymore. He was genuine and warm, trusting and friendly.

And then Aviva realized that she hadn't really known Yossi before, and it was her ignorance that had caused her embarrassment.

She had not allowed herself to see that Yossi was a caring, kind, *Yiddishe* boy.

"I made a poem for you," Aviva said, "to go with the gift."

She handed Yossi a card and pointed to the words as she read them.

"Yossi does *mitzvos*,
   he always will try,
to reach for the heavens,
   like a bird flying high."

"Like a bird," Yossi repeated, rubbing his glass bird.

"Like a bird," said Rabbi Diamond thoughtfully, "reaching towards heaven. With every *mitzvah* we do, every word of Torah we learn, we are always reaching towards *shamayim* and coming closer to *Hashem*."

Shaya's face lit up. "If we do that, we'll all be like real diamonds."

Avremele toddled over to Yossi and patted his cheek. "Ossi Di-mon."

Yossi tilted his head to the side and smiled happily. He knew he was just a little boy, but at the moment his heart felt so big and so full of love and affection.

He didn't know what the future held for him. But he did know that with people like the Diamonds around, he had a chance like everyone else.

Down's syndrome is a congenital defect of mental and physical development. There is no known medical treatment that can cure Down's syndrome, but with specialized education, most affected children can learn to look after themselves and to lead useful lives.

If we use our efforts and time with sensitivity and compassion to help build self-esteem and a good self-image, we can help a Down's syndrome child to maximize his mental and physical capacity.

Y. W.